REVERIE

A collection
of
short stories and poems

Sowparnika D Sivan

notionpress.com

INDIA • SINGAPORE • MALAYSIA

CONTENTS

ACKNOWLEDGMENTS

I first and foremost thank my family for granting me all the support I could ask for; for their constant encouragement, appreciation and the criticism which helped me improve. I am forever grateful.

Special thanks to my mother who after reading each story of mine, commented on those special aspects that no one else did,

To my father who has been my most reliable editor and my favourite reader,

To my sister who truly and genuinely loves my stories, even if it might be because I was the one who wrote it; you will always be the most special writer I know,

To all my dear friends, who read my stories and gave me feedback, your opinions were always treasured by me,

To all my teachers who recognised a possible aptitude in me and encouraged me.

I thank God for blessing me with these people, for showering me with luck.

Thank you readers, for taking up this book and giving these stories a bit of your valuable time.

Acknowledgments

With this humble attempt of mine, I hope all of you are entertained and that it is worth your time.

THANK YOU.

THE MAIDEN

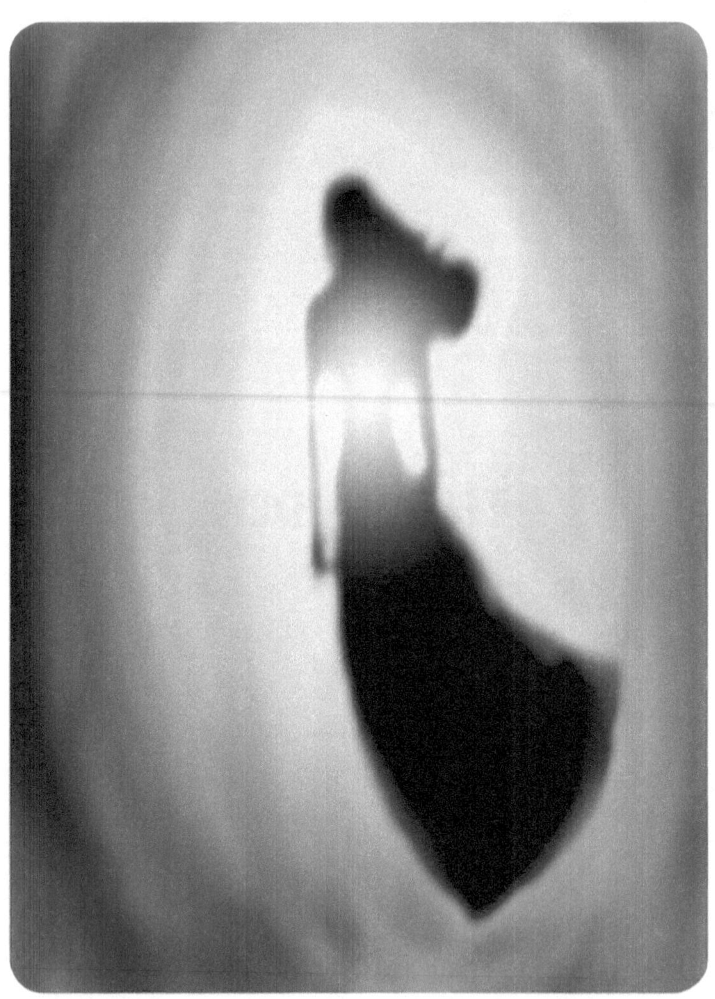

For those of you whose mind wander behind the strange beckoning.

———◆———

"At the heart of all beauty lies something inhuman"

— ALBERT CAMUS

Unnatural, blood curdling, horrifying. These were the few words to describe the incident which was now all over the news. The news of a suicide. That alone is enough to wrench an empathetic philanthropist's heart. However, what made this news unacceptable to even the most aloof members of the society, was not what had happened, rather who it had happened to; more appropriately, who had done it.

In this case the accused and victim were one. A six year old from the southern end of town, the last house of a street ending in a dead end.

"She is dyslexic". The doctor made his verdict. The mother of the diagnosed nodded. Time to arrange for a tutor. As far as I could predict, she wasn't particularly disappointed or worried. Dare I say.. excited? The mother was a social media influencer. Not the fancy, living the best life, brand ambassador model kind. She was one of those who spread awareness about positivity and acceptance. Accept your body, accept your feelings, love yourself no matter what. "Advocates of easy joy", my naughty term for them. Everything according to them is ok and meant to be accepted. For them, the people who aren't flawed like them are unnatural, unacceptable.

The little girl was sitting beside her mother; the latter had millions of reel ideas fleeting through her mind about the flaw in her child, a subject for her to yet again "embrace". The child wanted to go home… and draw some more.

"Every child is special! Its nothing short of a mesmerising delight to see them unfold their own unique personalities! This was one of the drawings my daughter made… It was so spontaneous!! That too on a random newspaper…!"

The mother was filming, holding up a painting done on a page of the newspaper by the little girl. It was a brilliant blend of colours, each unconventionally complimenting the other, to form a silhouette of a lady, against a bright hue of yellow and orange. A maiden walking from the open doors of heaven; that was the lofty interpretation made by the mother, and hence all her social media followers. But I for a fact knew, that the little girl had something else in mind while producing that masterpiece on the dichromatic dull canvas of black and white.

The child was now visible in the background of her mother's video; her ambidextrous hands working on yet another newspaper. It was another one of her paintings of the said maiden.. too early to decide what it was.

But drops of water steadily fell onto the wet paint.

When her mother would be done filming, she would finally become cognizant of her daughter's weeping. On repeated and concerned questioning but with no answers, she will start her own investigation… opening up her school bag and rummaging until she finds a spelling test paper with harsh remarks by a teacher. She finalises that as the reason for the blots of saline liquid adding a serendipitous allure to the new painting and proceeds to reprimand the hostile behaviour of the teacher who failed to remember to accept her child's drawback and subsequently embrace it like she liked to preach about. That incident too would soon make way in to her social media page.

It was only I who knew what the little artist was crying for…

***

The police and media reporters were hustling about in the household, which was usually well kept, tidy, bright and posh; now still posh and tidy, but suffocating with the dreadful reality. The mother was getting interrogated, her usually confident flowery demeanour now replaced by a terrified disbelief. Her child had committed a suicide. For all the scepticism I have for her ideologies, I couldn't help but sympathise with her terrible misery. Unable to come to terms with the unbelievable truth, spiralling into the depths of angst for the possibility of peccancy for the whole incident, fear of being framed as a hypocrite who sermonises in social media but sins in real life, and the most looming of them all, the excruciating pain of losing an innocent child to the most heinous death. My heart did reach out for her.

"Are all these her paintings?" One of the investigators questioned, pointing to a bulk of painted newspapers strewn across the marble floor.

A demented nod was the response.

"Did she only draw on newspapers?"

"Yes.. We got her so many books and bundles of canvas, but she never used those."

The investigators returned their focus to the paintings. Unbelievably good to be the creation of a six year old. Dyslexia does have a history of creating excellent art. In this case, all the pieces of the excellent art were that of a maiden. From different angles, in different scenarios. Each had something in them that led most viewers believe it was a heavenly message. The maiden an angel, walking out of heaven in a page, tiny red roses dropping from her seraphic hands in another; her angelic body levitated, her eyes towards the heavens, her hands below her face; grasping a prayer in their yearning effort, in a third. Somehow, the background of the plain letters of the newspaper added an unsettling effect.

"Sir?", one of the assistant investigators called out to his senior.

He looked at the latter, apprehensive concern in his face,

"She only drew on newspapers… and only on the same page of each newspaper.."

The senior bent down, peering not at the art, but at the unsettling canvas.

True enough, all the paintings of the little artist were done on the obituary page of the regional newspaper.

✳✳✳

We were at the funeral. It was a pretty crowded one, given the mother's popularity and the extent to which the news horrified people. They are right.. it takes something petrifyingly satanic, to influence such a child, God's little lamb, to commit something gruesome and beyond their innocent capability.

The child was to be cremated. Her serene pale face a reminiscence of the serious child she used to be. Her small chubby hands, still seemed to be at work with paint… the scars at her wrist, the last and deadliest of her artworks.

I wondered where her paintings were. I desired them to be burnt along with her body, but they were protected as some possible evidence. But one day I will take them with me.

Especially the one where the maiden was thought to come out of yellowish light of heaven; but I knew it to be a lady walking into the depths of ravaging fire; the one where tiny roses were dropping from her palms; which in fact was blood draining out of her hands synonymous to life draining out of her body; the one where she was apparently caught in powerful prayer, but was actually desperately clawing at her throat, fallen victim to the invisible noose around her neck. All these beautiful but deadly paintings, made more beautiful by the stories of death printed on the child artist's favourite canvas. It is a relief that people saw the paintings through a window tinted with grace and pleasantry… they would not be as capable to appreciate the pictures of purposeful pursuits of death.

The body was now lit on fire.

I looked down, at the little girl holding my hands now, free from the prison of life. We walked, away from the generally cognizable reality.

You might wonder who I am?

Why..

I am the maiden in the little girl's paintings; the darkness that corroded her innocence…

MEMORIES THAT DON'T DIE

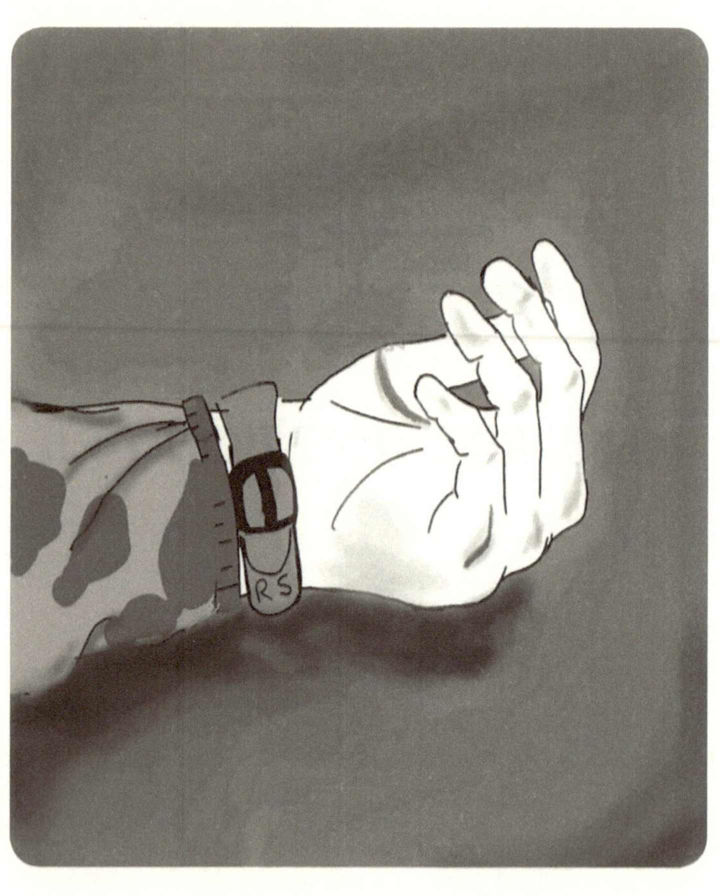
R S

For all the brave soldiers, and your selfless deeds, I cannot thank you enough, admire you enough.

"The tragedy of war is that it uses man's best to do man's worst"

– HARRY EMERSON FOSDICK

Beads of sweat slowly meandered down my temples, clinging on to the edges of my eyebrows for a hot moment before dropping as salty pearls. I could feel the heat closing around my face and the wetness of my shirt clinging to my back. I was trying to control my panting, and to stand straight.

"Punjaba-Sindhu-Gujarata Maratha…"

The group of students huddled around the mic sang; each chest heaving with meticulously inspired air in between verses; with the relief of having sung the previous and in preparation of having to sing the next. My throat was parched. My friends and I had to run to the assembly from the cricket ground, having to face our teachers' disapproval for our tardiness. With each passing moment, I could feel my mouth getting drier and drier. I glanced around. My math teacher, a middle-aged man with greasy parted hair and unevenly shaved face glared at me.

"Tava shuba name jage…"

He was mouthing the words aggressively, his wide eyes sending me an intense message, spittle spewing through his bottle brush moustache. I realized I wasn't singing the anthem, like I was supposed to. I took a deep breath and joined the chorus.

My eyes opened lazily. I could see shades of red; from light tones to dark ones, the world was a beautifully painted canvas. I blinked for a few times, with the calm joy of being able to witness something beautiful filling inside of me.

And my world went upside down.

A heavy boot pressed down my back and lifted, crushing my ribs. Everyone was running around, in a chaotic frenzy, stampeding the fallen soldiers. Pain as I have never known before, strangling and suffocating me. I could feel my body's desperate effort to maintain its functioning.

This was it, I thought to myself. A few more gasps to the ultimate surrender. I let the pain engulf me; the shooting stabs on my left thigh, the crushed torso, the looming emptiness to the left of my face. Did I lose an ear? I didn't have the courage to drag up my hand and find out. It didn't matter now anyways. My eyes closed and my cognizance faded once again.

I was hiding behind the old cupboard in my maternal grandparent's house, excitement encouraging my heartbeats. With a toy gun in my hand, I was waiting for the opportune moment to reveal myself and attack them. I had been waiting for 30 seconds. I had to use the washroom, urgently. Those unfortunate situations when you have to stay absolutely still, but then the apprehension makes your heart beat really fast, making your bladder lose its resilience with each passing moment. I had to keep fidgeting my legs and the consternation of whether those movements will give away my hiding spot was incredibly vexing. There were still footsteps, stomping upon the creaky floors.

I heard a distant squeal, and then the vigorous clicking of the toy gun followed by a gleeful chortle. One of my cousins had shot down another. There were sounds of cackling and scurrying which got fader and fader. This was ideally the opportune moment, to go behind them and attack. One could shoot down another while the latter was still in the shock of the assailment. Sadly, the situation was not ideal and I had to attend nature's call. However triumphant I would be if I could defeat all my cousins, it wouldn't be worth the embarrassment of a pool between my legs. I tiptoed up to the washroom door. The sight of the toilet bowl further exhilarated my bladder into the hope of immediate relief. I threw down my gun and dashed in with the panic of urgency. I sighed in relief as the sound of gurgling rivers filled my ears.

A sudden clicking noise from behind. I froze in dismay.

"Hands up!"

A loud gunfire shook me rather harshly into alertness. My oath to resignation of life ended there, though not voluntarily. I kicked back and rolled out of the way, the desperation to keep living overpowering the protests of my damaged limbs. The sheer loudness of the world set in. Gunfire, missiles, screams, heavy footfalls all diluted into one other making it merely an annoying bee's buzz. A bee's buzz that was deafening. I dragged myself away. I didn't have any desired destination in mind. Anywhere but the loud gunfire, anything but the loud gunfire. I reached a reasonably huge mound of debris. I sought shelter under the weak disintegrable shade. There was near zero possibility that the debris mound would protect me. Still, anything but the loud gunfire.

Elbows and knees deep in muck, I was scrawling below the net. The training sessions had begun about 8 months ago. At that instance when I was struggling to breathe with the sun beating down the back of my neck mercilessly, I realised that no measure of patriotic ambition could have prepared me for this torment. I was panting for my life, each inhale giving me another bout of nausea from the stench of the wet mud. I wanted to give up. The net rose slightly above my head and was lowered again, letting in an alluring breeze of fresh air. Good lord! Someone seemed to have finished the track and got out. The peer pressure set in and I started moving with renewed energy. I raised my head ever so slightly so that my chin was just barely touching the mud. The ending was near. With a sense of triumph, I pushed forward faster. With the renewed motivation, my regards for self-preservation was simultaneously lowered. My right elbow slipped and I crashed face down into the smelly dirt. I immediately pushed myself up along with the net coughing and spluttering the distasteful mud in the starkest disappointment. I heard laughter around. My fellow trainees who had finished the track were looking at me and guffawing, some tottering a little due to the effort and after effect of the exertion of the training. Some could hardly stand straight. I felt a giggle forming from my chest. I laughed getting rid of majority of the insect ridden dirt out of my mouth and swallowing the rest.

I smiled at that memory. I started laughing. Raucously, full heartedly, unapologetically. This was definitely my last day on earth. My last moments may as well be in good humour.

Suddenly, the loudest blast shook the entire ground, killing my carefree glee ruthlessly. I was robbed of the nostalgic delectation in violent abruption. Only the periphery of the mound blew away from the impact, indicating the relative proximity of the blast.

THUD

An arm fell next to me. A detached dusty bloody arm, right next to my face. I scurried back in shock, alarmed to my core, unable to stomach the gore. The arm wore a black watch, now it looked like a crown on a head. I looked away, simply because I couldn't stand the sight.

That's when I realised. I stopped breathing. I had to look again. I had to see a last time, to make sure. I turned my head with difficulty and once again looked at the picture of war. A titan leather strap, the fading initials of a name that was no stranger to my tongue. The pain set in again. This time, the wave of overpowering grief washing me over, so strong that my physical pain seemed superficial. I felt the traces of tears leaving traverses of coolness on my face, my lungs struggling with every wail of despair. I couldn't take it anymore. I wanted it all to stop. I reached out for the hand, the hand that pushed me in zealous teasing, patted my back in encouragement, and held me when I was downhearted. I held the arm and its memories tight, close to my bloody chest. Waited.

Time was cruel, I looked back and I could see my whole life reduced to seconds, yet these moments where I waited for my last breath to leave my shell of a body seemed like forever.

A grenade landed next to my feet. I felt as if my torso wouldn't allow the effort. Then I realised that my heart wouldn't allow the idleness. I reached out, pain blinding me, and I closed around and enveloped the small insignificant object bound to end significant lives; with a hand that held my favourite memories close to my chest.

"Jana gana mangala daayaka jayahe.."

It would end soon. I raised my voice to sing louder, more to satisfy the math teacher than to quench my sudden patriotism.

"Jayahe! Jayahee, Jayahee..

JAYA JAYA JAYA JAYAHEE!"

The last word was shouted in urgency by the assembly, some already reaching for their bags while singing so. I was among those some. I reached for my bottle and gulped down in greed.

Relief...

THE MORSE CODE

*For the two most important people in
my life, a love story like yours is yet to be
written*

———————◆—◆—◆———————

*"Love is like the wind, you can't see it, but
you can feel it"*

— *NICHOLAS SPARKS*

PROLOGUE

Walking towards the big, desolate ground, to see someone whose bewitching charm emanated a fortuitous welcome in the bleak area, I had the familiar excited thump in my heart, which added delightful exuberance to my senility. I cursed my wobbly legs and my degenerating lungs that failed to match the enthusiasm of my desires. I was getting closer to her, to finally talk to her. Moreover, today was extremely special, her birthday.

I could see my destination, I started practicing what I had to tell her first; with my fingers. Morse code was our favourite form of communication.

"Happy birthday my shamrock…"

My wrinkled hand was excitedly thumping and scratching on my pants.

I reached.

I saw her, smiling at me through the framed photo.

I bent down and kneeled with effort, my eyes brimming, not with protests of being cruel to my old body with my eccentric ambitions, but with overwhelming love.

I tapped and scratched on the smooth slab of her grave, wishing her what would have been a happy 75th birthday.

I proceeded to tell her more, what had happened over the week; how my invasive nurses would reprimand me for kneeling down right now with my fake knee cap ready to betray me any second; and how I would rather lose function of all my joints, fake or real (except my fingers of course) than let go of an opportunity to tell her that I love her.

In that vast cemetery with its eminent emptiness, I took my time with my morse code on my shamrock's grave, making the other rested souls envious of our love, always alive no matter what.

SHAMROCK

The day of cultural fest at our institution, and I was to sing a song. It was the last thing I wanted to do, but the nun would not have it any other way. Every child was to perform. I tried a negotiation tactic where I asserted that a 23year old could hardly be called a child and hence I should be excused from performing this year too. The nun remained illogically and irritatingly stubborn. Sadly, I did not have the courage to point out those character traits to her and had to succumb to her fancies. The media persons were loitering, capturing various performances of the students. I knew that the reporters and journalists there didn't see us just as students performing. They saw us as disabled people having our own go at life. Next day in their channel, they would broadcast clips of these performances, there, honouring us with the fancy term of "differently abled" and showing to the world the wonders we can achieve, like singing "Silent night" horribly out of tune. I managed to stay out of this for the past 3 years. There is only my brilliant manipulation skills and creativity to thank. This year, I had a set back, and the consequences were dire.

The audience probably didn't care that I couldn't get a musical note right for the life of me. All they would see is a blind girl doing something on stage. That alone ticked the criteria for being "extraordinary". But why did I have to be extraordinary?

Little Maria's dance got over, she received tearful applauses; more for her lack of arms than for her effort. A rendition on piano, a speech, a group dance and it was me.

I was sweating with apprehension.

Getting restless, I started tapping nervously on the table, first listlessly, then in the strange pattern of morse code.

I was repeatedly forming the same pattern

"I don't want to do this.. I don't want to do this".

"Then don't do it"

I heard a tapping that was not mine.

I immediately felt myself retracting into my skin. Who was it? Where was the person? How long were they there? Why are they watching me?

It was the familiar panic of being aware that I was an easy victim.

"Im sorry.. didn't mean to startle you".

A slower and seemingly sympathetic tapping ensued.

My face would have reflected my fright. I was still unsure about this stranger who was apparently well practiced in morse code. Probably not as good as me, but better than other people I know, who aren't even aware of such a language.

"Are you here to perform?" I tapped back, still apprehensive.

"Im guessing vision is what you lack. Im a 28 year old man who looks 40 and perpetually disinterested. Its been 12 years since I have been asked to perform."

"If vision isn't what you lack, you can tell fate has been kinder to you than me. Im 23 and Im expected to sing a Christmas carol in the mid of March in about 15 minutes"

I was getting over my anxiety of the unfamiliar event.

"Do you sing well?"

"Horribly is an understatement."

"Then for the first time in my life, Im glad Im deaf".

The mic announced my name, and an encouraging applause followed. That was my first time walking to that cursed stage with a smile on my face, and a giggle my new friend couldn't hear.

Once I was done, I went back to the table; and a morse code told me that as a deaf person, it was difficult to watch too.

I had to withdraw my assumption of him (I confirmed his gender from the way he sneezed) being not as good at morse code. He was solely dependent on his sight to assimilate the sentences, interpreting the gap between dots and dashes just through his vision.

✳✳✳

It had been a month since our unplanned rendezvous.

Ward number 27 of block 3, that place had taken authority of my thoughts. I was told that the gate to the block was 56 steps away, and the entrance an additional 21 steps. Then there was a gradual upward slope, a double door to the left. 16 steps and face towards your right, that would be number 27.

I just decided not to blindly trust his formula; given that he was taller and therefore his calculated number of steps not accurate for me, and that he wasn't blind, making him oblivious to the cautions that a blind person would have to take.

The helpers usually take us whichever new place we want to go within the campus. However, I decided against taking the help from an orthodox helper to meet a man. A man I liked, a real one whom I knew in person, after a parade of infatuations on singers I listened to on radio.

One day, when the weather was pleasant and we were taken to the park, he took me to the seesaw. I was flustered and confused if he was asking me to play with him. Thankfully, he was aware of his age and the societal expectations of adults. He only took me there because the wooden seat of the seesaw would prove an excellent pad for morse code.

That day, I demanded to hear his voice. He kept denying at first. When the morse code failed to render the attempted bullying effective, I resorted to the means of getting sympathy.

"Sound is my main facilitator to not just exist, but live in my surroundings, and sight is yours. You get to see me, but I don't get to hear you. Not fair"

So he spoke.

"Hello Shamrock"

His first words to me. His speech was made with effort, his words blunt. Born deaf and with a defective larynx, a low paid speech therapist was his only means to understand talking. Each word he said sounded like it was in a bubble, or balloon. Some kind of membrane separating his words from clarity. His voice was strange, eliciting a feeling a practiced instrumentalist would have if suddenly the strings of his violin got loose.

In my teenage desires, my knight in shining armour was a singer, his voice would be like the transition from twilight to dusk, smooth and ethereal. I always thought a dreamy voice would form the story of my love, if at all it was to happen.

The man near me couldn't be farther away from what I thought, but his fingers tapping and sliding was my new melody.

I first considered telling him that by words, letting him read my lips to make the occasion special. Thankfully, I decided against that.

Conventional speech was not special to us, it was for the rest of the world, and I was tired of trying to do things like how the rest of the world, the "normal" people did.

A few days later, my morse code flustered than usual, confessed my feelings, and his morse code reciprocated.

✳✳✳

"I can see some wood shamrocks by the walls"

It had been over 6 years since we started romancing, and the nickname he made for me completely replaced my real one. His reasoning was that, like wood shamrocks I was pretty, but with closed petals. My eyes never open to see the beauty of the world, but the world sees me as beautiful.

Last time I saw myself, I was buck teethed with wild hair and a big nose. Once I asked him to describe my face.

"Strong eyebrows, a big cute nose, lips like the butterfly pea flower covering teeth that threaten to tell tale about your buck toothed past. And ironically, eyes so big that the earth could fit in it. All big things but in a small face, framed by hair that's almost curly"

After that long session of tapping and scratching, I felt blissfully loved. He didn't usually tell me that I was beautiful except for rare occasions, but even when he described my flaws, I felt like he truly loved my face.

"Get me a shamrock" I tapped on the book he brought with him.

I heard him getting up and the fading sound of his footsteps. Botany was his favourite subject. He was intensely academic, learning every subject that was available in our curriculum and library. A "normal" person in his place would have by now been highly accomplished. He was pretty good at sports too. Drawing not so much. Singing was an obvious no.

I remember few years back when he told me why he gets so consumed in such pursuits.

"I am not normal, I have a liability. As a child, when they used to show us movies and shows about Hellen Keller and a hundred other prodigies, I always used to believe that I belonged among them; there has to be something in my life that makes it an

extraordinary accomplishment. I thought I would be a picture of inspiration. So I did whatever I could, studied furiously, played basketball no matter how many times I embarrassed myself, hoping to see myself in inspirational movies one day. I even tried playing a piano until I realised how pointless it was for me. Whatever I did, I was very good at, but not extraordinary enough for some rich dude to sponsor a good future. When I was young, I somehow always seemed to dodge the adopters' eyes. Luck played hide and seek with me and I always lost. I'll be just a deaf guy who comes with no additional packages of inspiration".

Listening to that sad finger code, I felt helpless. Do I convince him to keep trying, or do I offer him the smarter advice to accept the reality. I could have told him that in my eyes, he was extraordinary, but that probably wasn't what he was looking for.

Back to present, I felt a warm hand open mine and drop something cold and delicate. The smell of fresh dewy flowers.

"Its okay, I'll do that myself".

I told my friend, a young lady with down syndrome who was helping me get ready for the wedding. She was reaching up to attach a brooch to the top of my wedding dress. My wedding dress was just a white plain long frock with sleeves. It was a new one, the first one I bought on my own selection since I was admitted to the institution. The wedding was a secluded one, with just the mentioned young lady and a few friends of his as witnesses. No one to officiate. We had first told our Mother Nun about it, with her circle of administrators. They had eventually come to accept us being together though they scathingly disapproved. We were treated like an ugly birthmark, they didn't like us together, but couldn't really do anything about it. Over the years, I stopped giving a damn about the helpers and nuns and was spending majority time at ward 27. But when we put forward the idea of marriage, we didn't receive any help from the board. They were incredulous and ridiculed us passively about our form of communication. Hence, we decided to do it by ourselves, not like the rest of the world with priests to officiate. But, we hardly did anything like the rest of the world did.

I was now 41, he 46. We married because, what else was there for us to do?

We had lots of discussions about it before too.

"I cant have children".

I once told him. The accident when I was 12 had affected my uterus too, along with taking away my sight. I was scared of telling him that. I already felt bad enough that he couldn't do anything he dreamt of, and I was worried that he wouldn't find a family that he wanted with me either.

"I know"

"Don't you want a family? A truly "normal" family at least?"

For a while, there was no tapping.

"God intended us to be abnormal. For others, falling in love through morse code is absurd… for me, it has been the most natural thing. I don't want to be normal anymore. We are destined to be strange together"

When I walked down the supposed isle (actually a corridor in front of the ward 1 dormitory), with a wooden slate in my hand to tell my vows, I thanked God for making us abnormal.

"I love you shamrock",

He told me both in morse code and his lovely voice.

✳✳✳

Last stage of leukemia, the diagnosis was made late too. Thankfully, I didn't suffer much, days with him were never sorrowful. Of course, our marriage was not all devoid of fights. My favourite way of making him more infuriated was to stop the morse code and call him some choice words making sure that he could read my lips.

The making up would be again in morse code. Lately, I have been talking more and tapping less, credits to the syringes that decorated my hand. It was unfamiliar talking to him, and it made me feel despondent. But he always had something to tell me in morse code that would just about make me forget all the worries.

I could sense that I was currently on my death bed, the very last stages. My palm felt the wetness of a wrinkled face. He was now old, handsome still at 68 years old as far as my touch would tell me. We spent exactly 40 years with each other, and often times I wondered if God was teasing me, giving me so much joy through such unlikely means.

"I've not had enough of your lame humour. Promise to keep telling me, visit me at my grave."

"I promise"

I heard sniffing and weeping.

"I'll be kind and give you about 8 days to mourn, after that you should be happy again, and tell me more stories. It would be such a bother having a gloomy husband down here when Im trying to enjoy heaven".

"Your husband is gloomy because he has a good reason to worry that heaven might not be where you find yourself"

Rude of him to make me take the effort to laugh. After a brief silence, I heard more tapping.

"I was wrong. I am not just a deaf person with nothing special."

More pause.

"You gave me something that not even the normal people could dream of achieving. It is too good for the world to know. Like the most promising treasure, but only we could discover it.

Im not just any deaf guy. You are my extraordinary accomplishment shamrock"

I could feel myself leaving the earth. He was wrong to be worried; I was already in heaven with his last morse code for me.

EPILOGUE

At the cemetery behind the Institution for the Differently abled, a new coffin was lowered. Next to the one with a smiling photograph of a lady installed there by the one currently in the coffin.

13 years of solitude in conversing with morse code; now the heaven was about to witness the rhythm of love in dots and dashes.

SECRETS

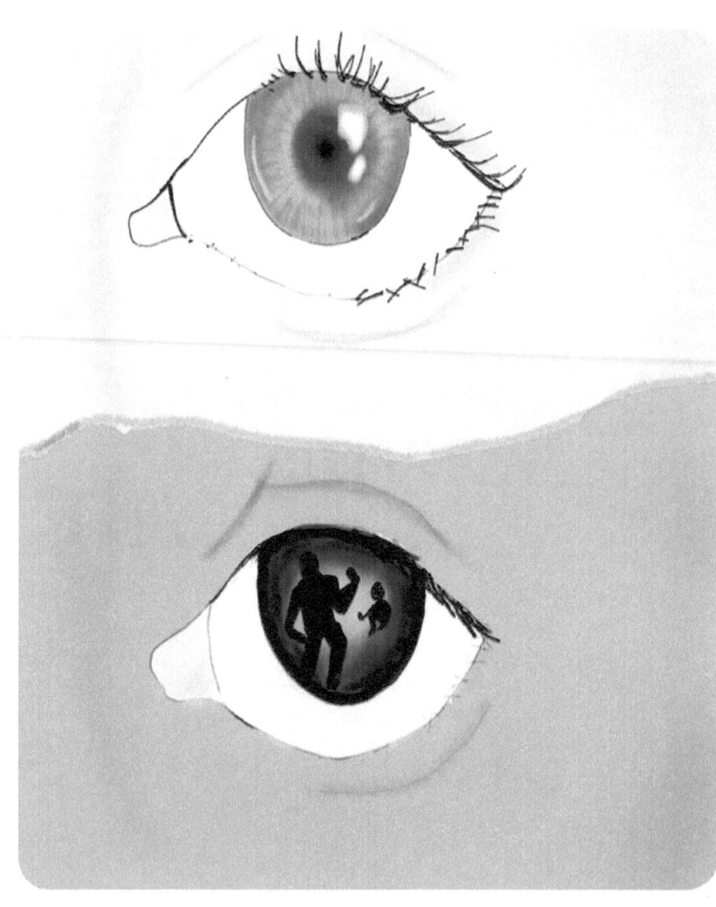

*For my closest kin, your mind is a wonder,
your heart a treasure*

———————◆◆———————

*"All secrets become deep. All secrets become
dark. That's the nature of secrets"*

– CORY DOCTOROW

"I can read minds"; her selcouth claim was met with admiration of her friends and sceptic disbelief of the rest. Which meant that everyone believed in her miraculous capability except me. Being popular had its rewards, for starters, people love you, they satisfy your hunger for attention and they believe you when you say that you can read minds. I always looked down upon them, her friends (more like her minions). The idea of mindlessly accepting and glorifying whatever she threw at them disgusted me. In all honesty, I wouldn't have looked down upon them if I was a part of their friend group too; I too would have gleefully ooh-ed and aaah-ed at all her dramatics. Maybe the feeling of distasteful pity I developed for them was to console myself for not being accepted into their vanity circle. The self-instilled feeling of superiority made me forget about my incapability of being worthy of the popular group; so I obstinately disregarded everything they said and that helped me get a bit of attention to myself too.

"Read mine!"

That was the excited squeal of one of her minions. I snorted in haughty disbelief. As usual they turned their eyes on me. Each one of them looked offended and wronged, as it was each time I expressed my disapproval.

The queen bee looked at her minion, leaned forward and had up to eight seconds of intense eye contact.

"You are thinking of the colour blue".

The pompous statement was followed by another squeal and clapping of hands.

My sceptic disdain faltered, did she really know how to read minds?

They all turned to me and peered condescendingly.

"That's easy, everyone thinks of blue when they think of a colour".

"Some think red and green"

Counter arguments become futile attempts at desperate redemption when they are baseless, so I held my silence.

"Shall I try yours then?"

Her haughty gaze met my deceptive indifference. If I deny, I'll be acknowledged as a weakling and why would I allow that to happen?

"Go on". I drawled lazily.

Her wide hazel eyes locked into my small beetle like ones. A beautiful iridescent sunset meeting a plain colourless landscape. I often wonder if being beautiful is a necessary criteria for being liked.

"Hmm" she says with a knowing smirk.

My grandmother once told me:

A loving heart beats strong, a hateful heart beats weak;

An honest heart beats surely, a lying heart beats fast;

A tense heart beats lively, a peaceful heart doesn't beat at all.

My heart was beating fast, because it was lying, with secrets in its folds. Secrets not meant to lurk in a 10year old's tender heart. Secrets which sometimes made me feel special, and other times hateful of myself. Secrets nonetheless, their purpose in life is to continue living in the dark corridors of my mind, mildly festering, looming at me in my solitude, and dying with time; all in concealment.

What if she could really read minds? My heart started beating faster. I deliberately and repeatedly said the words in my mind, attempting at telepathy.

"Don't say it out aloud.. Make up anything, i'll agree with you"

My pitch black beady eyes, the only part of my face devoid of a deceptive clothing, stared into hers.

"She is revising the rule of tenses in her mind", she spoke decisively. Everyone looked at me expectantly, some daring me to deny, some curiously.

"Yes". With a well-executed raise of eyebrows and a mildly shocked tilt of head, I replied. Her chest rose in fulfilment, and she gave a proud smile to her minions who were thoroughly drunk in her magic. I searched in her eyes, for either a hint of surprise well concealed from the rest of her demeanour at me having complied to her fancies, or a look of dark demonly glee of having discovered something that can be used against me. But all I saw were the distant doll like eyes, beautiful in every way, but inhumanly emotionless.

Did she really know how to read minds? Did she see what is inside of me? The gory thoughts and the forbidden memories?

I'll never know.

THE LUNCH BAG

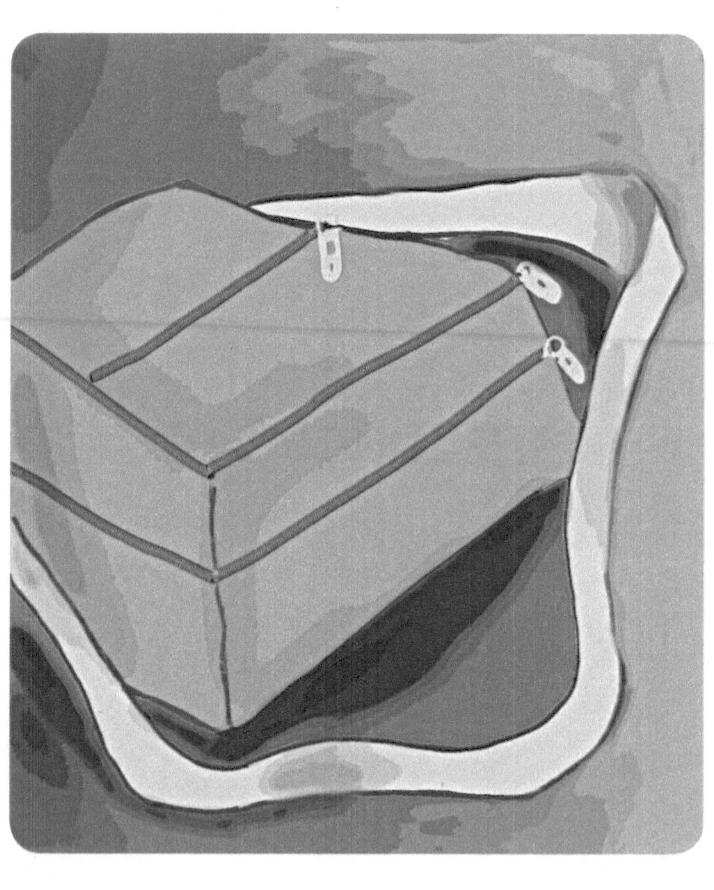

For the child in you and me; you are the best version of myself and always will be.

—◆—

"Innocence tinctures all things with the brightest hues"

– EDWARD COUNSEL

I sometimes accompany my mother to one of the houses she works at. These days, she is employed in a new one, a big one. Usually after school I would directly go with her; but nowadays it had been made mandatory for me to wash up before I went to that big house. Apparently, the owner of the house was a "big" man. One of those in coats with suitcases and shiny cars. So, I couldn't afford to be untidy. But he never saw me, he left early in the morning and came late at night; so, me tidying up was to probably impress his wife, though she hardly paid me attention after the first few days. She wasn't one of the fun ones. There were three types of "madams" that I knew:

1. Talks to me, gives me new chocolates and cakes, asks me to sing songs and lets me watch cartoon on the big TV.

2. Smiles politely, says hi but nothing more, sometimes treats me to left overs of delicacies.

3. A forced smile which is followed by a tempered whispering to my mother with furtive glances at me after which I am never taken to that house again.

The one in the big house where I go now was one of the 2nd type. Her daughter wouldn't speak much either; she was older and taller than me so she came back from her school in her fancy uniform later than me. I wondered if I would also be wearing the crisp blazers when I go to a higher grade. But the big students at my school just wore plain old shirt and skirt.

I wish the madam would invite me when she watched TV. Mother wouldn't let me loiter near the doors to catch glances of the big screen, saying it was unbecoming of me. So, I just followed her around, watching her sweep, mop, wash dishes, dry clothes and occasionally dust the cupboards. The first few days that she started taking me with her to the houses, I was excited to help her out; until one day I got too excited and knocked over a flower vase while scrutinizing the result of my mother's dusting by closely checking for any morsels of dust. After a frenzied panic and 2 stellar beatings on my bum, my mother picked me up rather harshly and deposited me away from the scene of crime. Like a hero, she went back in to clean the sharp glass pieces; though at that instance I thought of her as a rather evil lady who made cruel designs on my rear. Later, I was made to apologize to the madam with a tear-streaked face. She was one of the 1st types, and while some of you may consider it a good thing, I was absolutely ashamed that she out of all the other types of madams had to see me like that. She practically used to look up to me, always requesting me to recite the poems I learnt at school and waiting for my valued opinion of the food she made. I felt bad for her that she had to witness the downfall of someone she admired so.

After that, I never tried to help my mother physically. Although, I kept giving verbal guidance to her. Once, when she worked in the house of another madam of the 2nd type, I kindly pointed out to her that she was sweeping the dust under the bed and cupboards and not taking them to trash. That's when the madam came out of the nearby balcony and peered at us, assessing the situation. I thought I finally won her over, causing an upgrade from 2nd to 1st type with my brilliant observational skills. My mother never went to work there after that day, so I guess not. Hence my days of verbal advices were too forcefully put to an end.

It was a Friday and mother had to accompany the madam to the bazaar. I wasn't allowed on these trips and that was my biggest tragedy. I begged and pleaded every Thursday, yet on Fridays, I invariably find myself at my friend's house. At first, I was happy to be at my friend's, until one day, my mother returned with a toy. You pull its tail and it moved forward making a loud, rather obnoxious noise. It was like ones I never had before. I was thrilled. That day, I transitioned from being blissfully ignorant to a raving detective. Where was it that my mother went? In a place full of toys without me? Were there more toys of such kind that I could get? All these questions were burning my mind and soul. But mother wouldn't understand the intensity of my inquisitiveness, and every Friday I had to console myself with the company of my friend. He was the only one who understood my pain, my only source of empathy. He asked if I still had the toy. I told him I did, but couldn't carry it around lest its precious tail and its working be damaged. Taking sympathy to his desire, I told him I would show it to him when he visits my home and even let him have a go at pulling the tail, but only once. The glory of that promise produced an ebullient smile on his face. Affected by the contagiousness of it, I temporarily forgot about the sinfully forbidden trip to the bazaar.

That day she didn't come back with any toys or chocolates. I was hurt, but I consoled myself with an extra pull of the tail of the toy. Every day I was allowed only one pull, in accordance to my self-imposed rule that added sanctity to the wonderful toy. But the days when I was feeling under the weather, I would let myself have an extra pull, washing away my trauma with the toy's loud antics till it halts abruptly to inaction. Then, I pull myself back to reality from the brief period of bliss and brace myself professionally to handle the stings of life; like today. After the treasured extra pull of the day, I went to find my mother, to pester her with questions of where she went that day and what she saw.

Monday, after school, I was made to follow the new protocol and got tidied and clean to go to the house. There I followed my mother, telling her about school and how I decided that I would sacrifice a day of pulling the toy to let my friend do it. I also haughtily mentioned the discomfort I had to suffer throughout the day because of how she made my pigtails too tight that morning.

When the doorbell rang, I went along with mother to open the door. The madam's daughter handed her lunch bag and spared me a small smile and headed to her room. Usually, I smile back tentatively from behind my mother. Today was different. Her lunch bag was different. It was usually a plain cover that she fished out from a compartment of her school bag. Today, she had a whole separate tiny bag. Wonder filled my eyes. I ran behind mother to the kitchen, to watch her open the exotic object. A square bag with two zips running parallelly. Once you open it, you see yet another zip that opens to a cutlery compartment! The most delightful of it all, it was pink, my favorite color. I yearned to touch it and feel the pristine fabric. I discretely tried to offer my mother to help her take the cutleries out of the smaller compartment. A harsh rejection followed. I kept staring at it, intently and fiercely. After mother hung it over the hook, I stealthily let my fingers caress the sling of the bag. It felt new.

Once we reached home, I had my pull for the day and proceeded to do other less buoyant activities such as homework and learning the tables. After five minutes of learning I was convinced that I had completed the quota of hard work for the day and dilly dallied to indulge in more entertaining activities.

.At night, when I was laying on the mat with my mother's arm as pillow, the fumes from the mosquito repellant coil fogging the activity of my brain to slumber, I dreamt of the lunch bag, with its different zippers and compartments and its effervescent pink color.

Another day at school, another day of deep philosophical rumination about why there are so many different formats for English alphabets. Is there really a requirement for me to learn the capital letters, small case AND cursive? Once the teacher started going for rounds to inspect the accuracy of our writing, I told my friend about the bag I saw, explaining in detail and possibly adding a few fancy .appendages given the excellent audience he was being. They overheard me, the group I don't like. They started their hubristic claims of owning better bags and dismissing my descriptions of the pink lunch bag as purely fictional. I was appalled at their outrageous advances of calling me a liar.

I couldn't take it, and I said,

"I'll bring it one day."

That day I had to grant myself an extra pull; the stress was exhausting me. How would I get that bag to school and indefinitely buttress my claims?

***

The madam, her bigshot husband and the daughter were going on a 2day trip. It was a huge hustle; packing and cleaning the trunks. It was some big wedding, so all their fancy dresses that looked just like the ones that people in TV wear were to be packed in the suitcases. It was planned on short notice, so everyone was agitated. The madam was scolding my mother for something, I heard loud noises and went to investigate. My mother had her head down, the madam was actively gesticulating and shouting. Once madam saw me, she stopped momentarily. She continued in a lower voice, and this time she didn't smile at me. A burning feeling rose to my throat and wetted my eyes. But soon enough, mother took me to the kitchen garden and let me pluck a few chilly and I was ok again.

There were a lot of leftovers and it was packed in 4 boxes for mother to take. Happy that there would be something fancy to eat at night, I completely forgot about the earlier occurrence.

That's when the pink lunch bag again caught my eye, its undeniable allure sinfully encouraging me to commit chicanery. So, I did; in a rush of kleptomania, I took the bag and hid it in the one we were carrying the leftovers. It wasn't stealing! Just borrowing for a day. I would definitely return it once I put the self-absorbed nuisances in my class in their place. With my heart still beating about the illegality of it, I promised myself not to have a pull on my toy that day, to compensate for my temporary mendacity.

The next day was a holiday, so the day following, I would take the bag to school, make a visual announcement, and the next day return it when I come with mother. As of the current instance, I couldn't see any flaw in my carefully fabricated plan.

If only…

Flaw no. 1

My mother was to carry the bag of leftovers, what if she sees the object of theft inside?

I realized that when we were about to leave, and she reached for the bag. I had to insist on carrying the bag, till we reached home.

Flaw no. 2

Where would I keep it for a whole day?

.Upon reaching, I yet again had to find a good hiding place in that small barely furnished house of ours to keep it from my mother's sight.

Flaw no. 3

Having my mother drop me at school, wouldn't she still be able to see the pink lunch bag?

Again, I had to take out a few less important books from my school bag and replace it with the royalty of the lunch bag.

.My initial excitement was dying off, an unshakeable feeling of doom replacing it.

At school, I was waiting for the lunch break, period after period, my thumping heartbeat- the ticks of an unreliable clock.

Once the bell rang, I called the ones who questioned the credibility of my statements to the back of the class along with my friend, and whipped out the lunch bag.

Everyone was mesmerized, looking at it from every angle, watching me open the various compartments. I didn't feel the satisfaction of superiority as I had predicted, rather a looming anxiety was gnawing at me, especially when they started to feel it and working the zips for themselves. A teacher called me; I entrusted my friend, the one whose house I am at every Friday, with the safe keeping of the lunch bag and went to meet the teacher who had called me to insult my spelling abilities.

Once I was back, I saw one of the kids trying to fit his tiffin box in the lunch bag, without the worry of leaking curry staining the fabric. My friend snatched the bag with a "NO!", and that's when the hell unleashed. The bag scored against the edge of bench, a small gaping tear at the bottom staring at me. Punishment for the sin I committed.

Rest of the day passed in a haze, the gripping tension nullifying my normal functions. I reached home, didn't even think of my toy. My mother's smile seemed to sting, she would hate me if she knows what I did. I cried throughout the night, guilt squeezing my insides for dreaming out of my league, for pursuing something that could never be in my possession. When I slowly drifted to a disturbed sleep, a pink lunch bag came in my dreams, staring maliciously at me, the world closing in.

Next day, I felt feverish. Usually even if I felt minor ache on my knee, I would refrain from going to school. Today was different, I had to go, with the lunch bag, demoted in its glory due to my greed, in my school bag, so that when I go to the madam's house, I can restore it to its right place where it belonged.

We were to be at the house before the madam and her family arrived, preparing food and spurring the house which was inactive for two days back into liveliness. With more and more flaws revealing themselves, I gave up the hope of completing the little illicit project in perfect execution. However, nothing went drastically amiss, and when mother went to water the plants in terrace, I took out the lunch bag and hung it on the hook in a panicked frenzy.

But I knew that the worst was yet to happen, the madam will find out, she will shout at my mother once again like the day before the trip, and I will be taken away from home, to a monstrous place where bad children were put.

Later that day, I gave my toy to my friend to keep as his own after a last pull and made him promise that he too would only pull once a day unless a second pull was inevitable. He cried a lot too after the incident, out of empathy for me and guilt of his clumsiness that caused the defect. Initially I was angry with him, now I wanted him to be ok again. Anyways, the happiness the toy gave me seemed undeserved now.

✳✳✳

The fever escalated, I was in a delirium for over a week and had to go to hospital. My mother didn't go to work for many days.

I once asked her why she went to work, to sweep and mop at different houses. Is it because the madams didn't know how to?

She told me that it was very important to make money, and by sweeping and mopping, she would get the money. Would she get any money now that she was beside me?

After two weeks, I recovered, still tired but good enough to go to school. I played and did my tables, the former better than the latter. Sometimes, I missed my toy, but along with it came the fading but still worrisome apprehension of my doom of the lunch bag that would end all means to my joy.

After 2 months or so, on a Friday, when I was at my friend's house and he let me have a pull on the toy that was now his, my mother came to pick me up with a bag in her hand. Excited and eager, I rushed to see what it was.

"It tore a bit at the bottom, so madam bought a new one for her daughter. She said you can have this one!"

The pink lunch bag once again found its way to be in my hands.

DRIPPING SWEET

For all kind souls who never hesitate to reach out a helping hand for the ones in need.

◆◆◆

"Poverty is a very complicated issue, but feeding a child isn't"

— *JEFF BRIDGES*

Reverie

A day of exploring the city of Goa, I found myself before the great Bom Basilica,

Scrounging through the streets for souvenirs, enjoying the rhythm of the roadside a cappella,

With my parents and sister, my 12 year old mind working the execution of next mischief,

An iron hold on the wrist by my mother put an end to my short- term ambitions much to my grief,

On the way to the entrance of the big church, wonder filling one's eyes about the cadaver inside,

The great soul, his goodness apparently keeping his corpse fresh as the day he died,

That's when I saw her, a tiny girl not more than 4 in age, in tatters and torn,

Roaming about in front of the church gate, with her older sisters who looked more forlorn,

Reaching out her little hand to strangers, hoping to feel the coldness of a coin or two,

Then her sister came, waving a hundred rupee note in glee, they all rushed to the ice cream truck about to move,

With an ice cream stick now in her hand, she looked the epitome of contentment,

Now she came towards us, clutching her dear ice cream stick, walking carefully on the fresh cement,

She saw us, and hid the ice cream stick behind her back before reaching out an empty hand,

66

Lest we deny her a few coins seeing the luxuries she was living in, the glorious ice cream a magical wand,

I saw the little girl, her eyes still holding the light of innocence,

Her serious face and outreached hands full of professional essence,

I felt hyper aware of my fancy clothes, and my satisfied appetite,

My tongue could never experience the same blissful taste of the ice cream she held,

Even if I bought the same one, because for me, it was an ordinary ice cream, nothing to be marvelled,

My mother fetched a 20 rupee note from her purse, and placed it on the little palm,

Asked her to get another ice cream of another flavour with a smile quite warm,

I couldn't smile at the little girl when she glanced at me with her big eyes,

I was shrinking, the justice and fairness of the world seemed all like lies,

My skin felt like an expensive cloak I didn't deserve, my father hand around mine, a priceless luxury,

I wondered about the people lying, stealing, cheating, murdering and committing perjury,

Some of them living in comforts, without having to hold on to an ice cream with dear life,

And this little girl, scabs blotting her tender skin, the joy of an ice cream evading a hungry night,

When I entered the church, and paid my respects to the venerated saint,

I couldn't help but question him if he was only but a silent witness, my faith going faint,

I exited the church, my eyes searching for the little girl and her out stretched palms ever so tender,

All I saw was drops of melted ice cream, the sticky sweetness a bitter reminder.

REGRET

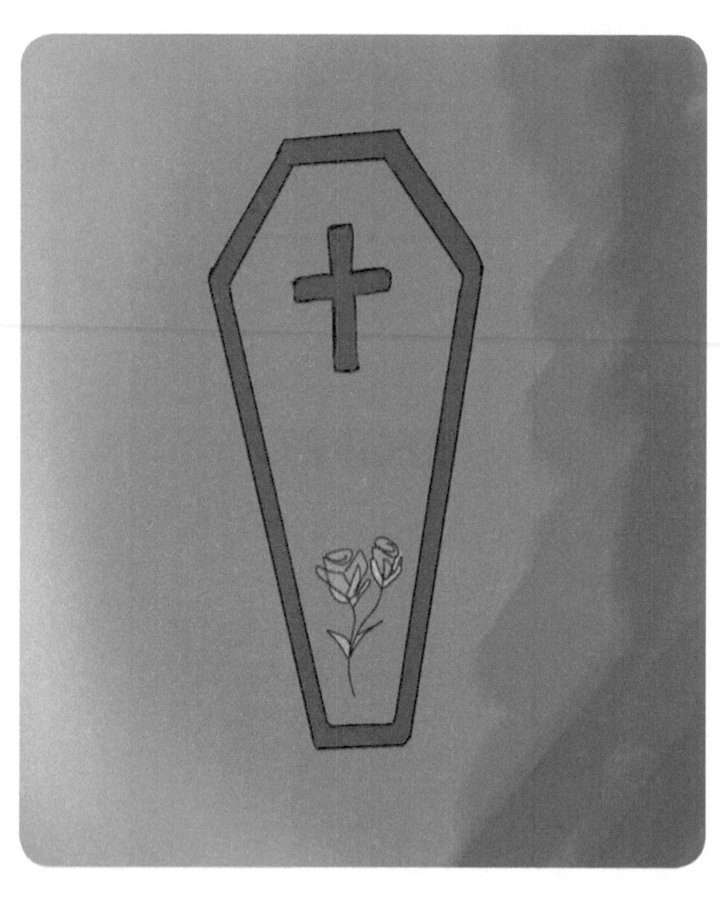

For my dearest friend, may you have all the happiness in the world and a little more.

"I'd rather regret the things I have done than regret the things I haven't done"

– LUCILLE BALL

An apology unsaid, a promise unkept,

The bitter tears unconsolably wept,

The eyes look but do not see

My soul reaching out, none to feel me

The ears hear but do not listen

My wretched cries; a cruel lesson

Superior to all, my hidden love

Then a propitious seed, now a lifeless dove

The soul yearns to say, to see, to feel

Those unsaid words, unseen beauty, unfelt glee

The love in me a serendipitous secret,

With life in me, I was busy but to fret

That sweet confession yet to be revealed,

In a coffin forever concealed.

The End